For Ameli
x x X

SIMON & SCHUSTER BOOKS FOR YOUNG READERS
An imprint of Simon & Schuster Children's Publishing Division
1230 Avenue of the Americas, New York, New York 10020
Copyright © 2007 by Emily Gravett
First published in Great Britain in 2007 by Macmillan Children's Books,
London.
First U.S. edition 2008
SIMON & SCHUSTER BOOKS FOR YOUNG READERS is a trademark of Simon & Schuster, Inc.
The text for this book is set in Aperto.
The illustrations for this book are rendered in pencil and watercolor.
Manufactured in China
2 4 6 8 10 9 7 5 3 1
CIP data for this book is available from the Library of Congress.
ISBN-13: 978-1-4169-5457-6
ISBN-10: 1-4169-5457-0

Monkey and ME

Emily Gravett

Simon & Schuster Books for Young Readers

New York London Toronto Sydney

Monkey and me,
Monkey and me,
Monkey and me,
We went to see,

We went to see some . . .

PENGUINS!

Monkey and me,

Monkey and me,

Monkey and me,

We went to see,

We went to see some . . . .

KANGA

ROOS!

Monkey and me,

Monkey and me,

Monkey and me,

We went to see,

We went to see some . . .

BATS!

Monkey and me,
Monkey and me,
Monkey and me,
We went to see,

We went to see some . . .

ELEPHANTS!

Monkey and me,

Monkey and me,

Monkey and me,

We went to see,

We went to see some . . .

KEYS!

Monkey . . . and . . . me,

Monkey . . . and . . . me,

Monkey . . . and . . . me,

We went . . .

. . . ZZZZZZZ.